Just
As Well, Really!

Written by Jillian Harker
Illustrated by Julie Nicholson

Bright Sparks ☆

Rumpus liked water.

He liked the drippiness and **droppiness,**

the splashiness and sloppiness of it!

He liked it so much that, whenever there
was water around…

...Rumpus somehow always managed to—

But Mom loved Rumpus, so

every time, she just sighed—and she mopped up the mess.

Rumpus loved mud.

He loved the way
you could

plodge
in it,

splodge
in it,

slide
in it and

glide
in it!

He loved it so much that, whcnever there was mud around…

...Rumpus somehow always managed to—

But Dad loved Rumpus, so

every time, he just sighed — and
he sponged off the splatters.

Rumpus enjoyed paint.

He liked to splatter and dash it,

to spread and splash it!

He enjoyed it so much that,
whenever there was paint around…

But Rumpus's brother loved him, so

every time, he just sighed—and he cleaned himself up.

Rumpus liked to find out how things worked.

He loved the prodding and probing,

the **wiggling** and the **jiggling,** the unscrewing and the undoing!

He loved it so much that, whenever Rumpus was around…

...things didn't work for long!

But Grandma loved Rumpus, so she just sighed—and she cleared up the clutter.

Rumpus loved his
mom, dad…

brother, and grandma…

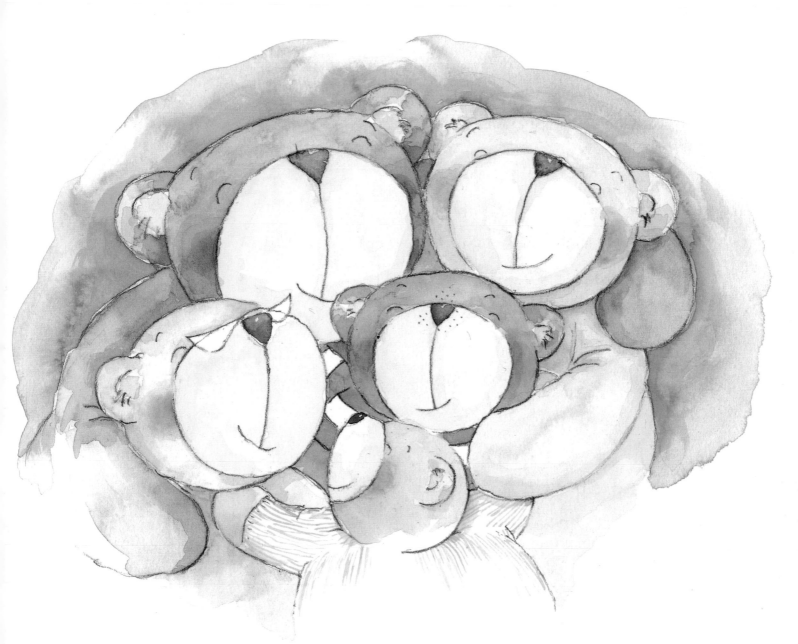

Rumpus's mom, dad, brother, and grandma loved Rumpus…

…just as well, really!

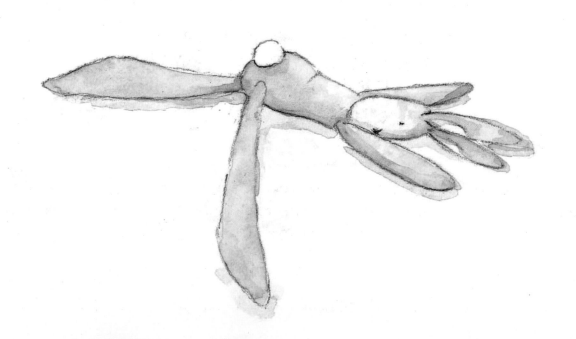